# A NEW ADVENTURE

Adapted by **CHLOE PEARCE**

MY LITTLE PONY and all related characters are trademarks of Hasbro and are used with permission.
© 2021 Hasbro. All Rights Reserved. Printed in the United States of America.
No part of this book may be used or reproduced in any manner whatsoever without written permission
except in the case of brief quotations embodied in critical articles and reviews. For information address
HarperCollins Children's Books, a division of HarperCollins Publishers, 195 Broadway, New York, NY 10007.
www.harpercollinschildrens.com

ISBN 978-0-06-303765-6

21 22 23 24 25  CWM  10 9 8 7 6 5 4 3 2 1
❖
First Edition

**HARPER**
*An Imprint of HarperCollinsPublishers*

This story is about a young Earth pony named Sunny.
Sunny loved hearing about all the amazing adventures
of Twilight Sparkle and her friends.
She didn't believe the scary stories about how Pegasi and
Unicorns once tried to eat Earth ponies and zap them with lasers!
Her dad had taught her that all pony kinds used to be friends.

Sunny knew that **ONE DAY** all ponies could get along again. So she decided to send a letter of friendship in a lantern, which floated high up into the night sky above Equestria.

**Then one day, a few years later . . .**

a **UNiCORN** arrived in town!

The ponies of **MARETIME BAY** were terrified and ran away in fright.

Hitch, the town sheriff, tried to capture the Unicorn. But Sunny knew this was her chance. She helped the Unicorn escape to safety.

The Unicorn's name was Izzy. She told Sunny that Unicorns can't shoot lasers. In fact, they don't have any magic anymore. Sunny's dad had been right all along! Sunny decided they should go to Zephyr Heights, the Pegasus City. Pegasi had magic, and maybe they could help bring the Unicorn magic back.

"But the Pegasi are bad news! They steal your sparkle!" said Izzy.
"What if you're wrong about them?" said Sunny.
"Earth ponies were wrong about Unicorns after all."
So they set off on their quest
to bring the magic back.

Meanwhile, back at the Sheriff's office, Hitch and his assistant, Sprout, were making a plan to find Sunny and arrest her. Hitch decided to go out and search for Sunny on his own while Sprout watched over the town.

But Sprout was very pleased to be Sheriff once Hitch had gone. He had plans of his own . . .

"The Unicorns could come back, and they could bring the Pegasi!" he shouted to the crowds. "We are all in danger! We must act now!"

His plan had worked. The ponies of Maretime Bay were scared and ready to fight the Unicorns and Pegasi.

On the road, Sunny and Izzy were soon captured
by two huge Pegasus guards!
   The guards put a tennis ball on Izzy's horn to try
to stop her magic and took them both to the city.

"Wooowww!" Izzy exclaimed—it was an amazing place
high in the clouds . . . and they had arrived on
the day of a ROYAL celebration.

The guards locked Sunny and Izzy in jail. But this wasn't like any jail they'd ever seen. It was more like a luxury spa!

Later, a Pegasus pony snuck in to set Sunny and Izzy free.
She was a Princess named Zipp.

Sunny and Izzy explained to Zipp that they needed help
bringing the magic back.

"I might have some information that could help,"
said Zipp. "Follow me!"

Zipp led Sunny and Izzy through a trapdoor and into a big hall. She told them the Pegasi had lost their magic, too. The royal Pegasi had only been pretending to be able to fly.

Then she showed them a huge broken stained-glass window above them.

"This was made a long time ago, when we still had magic," Zipp said. "That part shows the Pegasus crystal in my mom's crown."

This gave Sunny **AN IDEA.**

Sunny looked down at the broken shards on the floor and found a piece in the shape of a Unicorn crystal. It matched up with the Pegasus crystal perfectly!

"These two crystals belong together! Maybe if we reunite the crystals, then magic will return!" said Sunny. "And maybe all three pony kinds will get along again!"

Izzy and Zipp were amazed. The three ponies decided they would find the two crystals and bring the magic back.

Later at the royal celebration, as Zipp's sister, Princess Pipp,
was performing a concert, Sunny sneakily stole the queen's crown.

But then Pipp got caught up in the wires, and the crowd realized she couldn't really fly. It was a disaster! Suddenly, someone spotted Sunny and Izzy and shouted, "STOP! The prisoners are escaping!" as they ran for the exit.

The ponies managed to escape, along with
Princess Pipp, but not before running into Hitch,
who had come to arrest Sunny.

Sunny and her new friends explained that they were trying
to reunite the crystals and bring **MAGIC** back to Equestria.
Hitch and Pipp agreed to join them on their **QUEST**.

Their next stop was Bridlewood, home of the Unicorns.

Disguised as Unicorns, the ponies visited Alphabittle, who owned the Unicorn Crystal.

Sunny won the crystal in an epic dance battle.

**Sunny joined the two crystals together and . . . nothing happened!**

Sunny was confused and upset that her plan didn't work.
"I thought that I could make a difference," said Sunny. "I
don't know what I believe anymore. I guess this is goodbye."
Everypony was disappointed, and Sunny trudged back
home to Maretime Bay.

Later, when Sunny was packing up her old toys, she saw something sparkling under a night-light her dad had made for her. It was another crystal!

This gave Sunny an idea. Of course, there were *three* crystals, one for each of pony kind!

★    But in Maretime Bay, things had gotten out of hand. Sprout had made himself emperor and built a huge war machine. He planned to fight the Unicorns and Pegasi!

"Attaaaack!" shouted Sprout as he drove the machine forward. Sunny had to get help . . . and fast!

Sunny's friends soon arrived, but before they could join the three crystals, Sprout's war machine slammed into Sunny's home! There was a huge CRASH as the building tumbled down, with Sunny and her friends inside.

As the dust settled, all three pony kinds gathered round in shock. They began to help each other, making sure everypony was safe.

As Sunny slowly opened her eyes, she realized something MAGICAL WAS HAPPENING . . .

**As the Earth ponies, Unicorns, and Pegasi joined hooves,
a wave of magic spread throughout Equestria.**

The Unicorns and Pegasi
were amazed to find their
MAGIC POWERS had returned.

"I kept thinking we had to find the crystals to restore the magic," said Sunny, "but the crystals didn't need to come together. We did."